Girl Power

PRAISE FOR *STORYSHARES*

"One of the brightest innovators and game-changers in the education industry."
– Forbes

"Your success in applying research-validated practices to promote literacy serves as a valuable model for other organizations seeking to create evidence-based literacy programs."

- Library of Congress

"We need powerful social and educational innovation, and Storyshares is breaking new ground. The organization addresses critical problems facing our students and teachers. I am excited about the strategies it brings to the collective work of making sure every student has an equal chance in life."
– Teach For America

"Around the world, this is one of the up-and-coming trailblazers changing the landscape of literacy and education."
- International Literacy Association

"It's the perfect idea. There's really nothing like this. I mean wow, this will be a wonderful experience for young people."   - Andrea Davis Pinkney, Executive Director, Scholastic

"Reading for meaning opens opportunities for a lifetime of learning. Providing emerging readers with engaging texts that are designed to offer both challenges and support for each individual will improve their lives for years to come. Storyshares is a wonderful start."
- David Rose, Co-founder of CAST & UDL

Girl Power

Kitty Heite

STORYSHARES

Story Share, Inc.
New York. Boston. Philadelphia

Published in the United States by Story Share, Inc.

The characters and events in this book are fictitious. Any similarity to real persons, living or dead, is entirely coincidental.

Storyshares
Story Share, Inc.
24 N. Bryn Mawr Avenue #340
Bryn Mawr, PA 19010-3304
www.storyshares.org

Inspiring reading with a new kind of book.

Interest Level: Middle School
Grade Level Equivalent: 2.4

9781642611526

Book design by Storyshares

Printed in the United States of America

Storyshares Presents

1

Jaylin woke up and rubbed the sleep from her eyes. The small room was dark. She could hear people moving around outside of her door. She remembered what she had to do that day and felt a flutter of nerves run through her.

She crawled out of bed and crept to the door. Her twin brother Jonah was still asleep. It was good to let Jonah sleep since he was always so mean in the morning. She opened the door and looked out into the hallway.

People with puffy eyes walked down the hall with their toothbrushes. Bright lights shone down on them. Everyone wore gray shirts and brown pants. Even the walls were painted gray.

The camp was underground, so there were no windows. The only way to come in was through the warehouse above them. Many of the people in the camp had not seen the sun since they went underground before the war.

Jaylin moved into the flow of people as they went to the mess hall and the bathrooms. Adults and teens shuffled along together. Some chatted quietly about their plans for the day. Other people walked softly.

Jaylin went into the cafe to eat. It smelled of oatmeal and eggs. This room was also brightly lit and painted grey. The whole camp was the same. After so many years, the people in the camp were just used to it. Still, sometimes Jaylin had dreams about green grass and flowers.

Jaylin saw that only a small bit of sugar was put in each bowl of oatmeal. She wondered if they would run out of sugar soon. Jaylin took a small bowl of oatmeal. She wasn't very hungry.

"Jay! Over here!" A voice called to her from a few tables away. Jaylin looked up and smiled. Marcus was waving at her. His big smile was shining out from the grey and brown that surrounded him. He was sitting next to their other friends: Leila and Mike.

Jaylin, her twin brother Jonah, Marcus, Leila, and Mike had all grown up together in the same part of the city. They had gone to school together. Their families went to the same church and lived near one another. When the war started they all took refuge in their church together. Now they lived in a camp for survivors of the war. The five had become family. At 20, Jonah and Jaylin were the oldest.

"It looks like the sugar is running out," said Jaylin as she put her tray down next to Marcus. "There's definitely less than last week."

Marcus rolled his eyes. "They're just getting nervous. Jimmy was complaining yesterday that the Command was getting on his case about food. But they don't need to worry."

Marcus and Leila worked for Jimmy, the chief of supplies. They kept track of the camp's food, clothes, dishes, and water. Everyone in the camp had a job.

Everyone was expected to work hard. There were 2,000 men, women, and children in their camp, and they all needed to try to survive underground until it was safe to come out. Some were soldiers, but most were normal people.

2

Jonah came over to them with his tray. He was glaring at everyone at the table. He always looked angry before he ate breakfast.

"Good morning, sunshine!" Marcus said loudly. Leila and Mike began to giggle and look at Jonah.

Jonah just started eating his oatmeal. "There's not enough sugar. It tastes like cardboard," he said. He stared down at his bowl.

"That's because it is cardboard. Don't tell anyone. We've run out of oatmeal. We are all eating cardboard now." Marcus could not keep from laughing loudly as he said this.

Jaylin gave a small smile and looked away. Marcus always made jokes about running out of food. Jaylin did not always think it was funny.

"I'm going out today," Jaylin said suddenly.

Everyone stopped laughing.

Jonah put down his spoon. "What? Why didn't you say anything?" he asked. "Tell them no. Tell them to send someone else." He looked even angrier than he had a moment ago.

"It's my turn. I have to go," said Jaylin. She looked at her brother. She could tell he was scared for her.

"Who's going with you?" asked Marcus. He also looked scared. Across the table, Leila and Mike were staring at Jaylin with wide eyes.

"Sierra and Mary. We're the only ones who haven't been out yet," Jaylin said. Marcus closed his eyes and rubbed his face.

"I don't like it. I'm going to talk to your boss," Jonah said and started to stand up.

"No, it's my turn. I have to go someday." Jaylin put her hand on his arm to stop him. Jonah sat down, still looking angry.

Jaylin worked in Procurement. Her job was to go out of the camp and get more supplies. The camp always needed food, batteries, clothes, and medicine.

Only small people were chosen for Procurement. They had to fit into the special cars the camp used to go look for useful things. Every month a team of three Procurement workers went out.

Sometimes they did not come back.

Girl Power

3

After breakfast, Jaylin and Marcus walked to the Procurement team base.

"Why didn't you tell us sooner?" Marcus asked.

"Because I knew Jonah would try to change my job. I really want to do this," Jaylin said.

"You are crazy. I don't know why you want to go out there," said Marcus. "I just hope you come back. I'm going to worry the whole time. You're my best friend."

Jaylin saw tears in his eyes. She took his hand. "I have been training for almost two years." Jaylin reached her face up to Marcus's cheek and gave him a kiss. "I promise I'll be careful."

Marcus hugged her and held her close. "I love you, you know. I can't think how I would feel if something happened to you."

Jaylin felt her heart skip a beat. It upset her that Marcus was so sad. But she needed to go out with her team. Nothing could stop her.

* * *

Sierra and Mary were already at the Procurement base when Jaylin arrived. The three young women looked at each other. They knew they were about to do something scary.

They got their maps and their bags. The bags contained everything they would need to live for one week. After that, they had to get back to the camp.

"You need to look for power cells," said their boss, Captain Ross. "We think there are some here." He pointed to a large map.

Jaylin looked at the map. She could hardly believe it... there was a circle right around her old school. "Sir, I know that area," Jaylin said. "I grew up there."

"We know that. That is why we chose you for the team," said Captain Ross.

Jaylin's throat tightened. If she hadn't been scared before, she was now. What would she find when she went back home?

"Jonah tried to talk me out of it this morning," Captain Ross told her with a smile.

Jaylin was embarrassed. She knew her twin brother would try to change her team. It bothered her when he tried to take care of her like that.

The captain continued talking about the mission. "These cars are slow. They use electric power," he said. "If a trip took one hour before the war it can take four hours in these cars. You can't speed."

Jaylin looked at Sierra and Mary. It would take almost eight hours to get to the city. Other teams had already searched all of the towns near the camp.

"And watch where you're going. Some of the bombs dropped during the war never blew up. They can still explode if you drive over them," said Captain Ross. "Watch out for Rovers, too. There are two groups north of here."

Rovers were groups of people left after the war. They were almost wild. They killed other people and took their stuff. They did not live in one place. They traveled around. That was why they were called Rovers.

Some of the Rovers had been injured in the war. People who had been hit with the gas lost skin or body parts. They didn't look like they could be alive anymore. They looked like zombies.

"And girls," Captain Ross looked at them seriously, "I don't need to remind you how important this mission is. Each one of the three power cells will give us enough power for a whole year. We need you to find them."

"Yes sir. We will." The three young women tried not to think about the Rovers as they got into their cars. The gates around the camp opened. For the first time in years, Jaylin saw the sun. It wasn't very bright, but it calmed her nerves.

But the green grass she had dreamed of was nowhere in sight. Soldiers and other people stood with guns pointing out of the fence surrounding the camp.

Jaylin, Sierra, and Mary drove away quickly. The radios turned on in their ears. Jaylin could hear Captain Ross giving orders to shut the gates behind them.

Girl Power

4

They drove for an hour south towards the city. All around them they could see the mess from the war. Empty, burned down houses lined the sides of the road. Sometimes there were signs of life. Some farms looked like they were still being worked on. Jaylin could see houses with large stone walls built around them.

The cars they drove were small with three wheels. They had room in the front for one person. The back was for cargo. It looked a little like a glass bubble with wheels. They did not go very fast.

Jaylin, Sierra, and Mary were looking for a safe house. There were houses that other teams had prepared with power and food. "Let's stop at the safe house near the road. The map says it's close," said Sierra. Mary and Jaylin agreed.

All three cars turned off the road and through a neighborhood. Jaylin thought that a few years ago kids had ridden bikes down that street. Now, it was just a mess of ruined houses.

The cars turned into the driveway of an old house. They had to hide the cars in the garage. Rovers came to the towns at night. The cars would get their attention.

The girls took everything out of their cars and went in the house. The windows were painted black so they could use the lights and not be seen outside. They turned on the heat and made lunch.

"Let me see that map again," said Jaylin. Mary pulled the map out of her bag and they looked at it carefully. Jaylin pointed at the circle around her old school. "That's where I went to school. And right next to it is my old church." She looked at the map and was lost in her memory for a minute.

"Is your family still there?" asked Sierra softly. "I don't know. Jonah and I were taken by the soldiers," said Jaylin.

"So were we," said Mary. "Dad left to find medicine for the baby. The soldiers came while he was gone. Sierra and I had to go with them."

Jaylin didn't know they were sisters. She looked at them closely. Mary was tall with dark hair, but Sierra had blonde hair.

"We had a farm," Sierra said. "But when the war started, we hid in the cellar. Then the baby got sick. Dad left to get help. The soldiers took both of us. We don't know what happened to our dad or the baby." Sierra looked sad as she talked about what happened.

"That's like what happened to us," said Jaylin. "I was in the church with Jonah, Marcus, Leila, and Mike. Our moms and dads were there, too. When the soldiers came we had to go with them. There wasn't room for all of us." Jaylin took a deep breath. It hurt to talk about that day.

"Let's sleep now," said Mary. "Then we can get up very early and leave." Mary called back to base and told them the plan while the others set up a place to sleep.

The three young women ate a plain meal of dried meat and crackers. Then they set an alarm and lay down.

Jaylin had a hard time sleeping. She knew they would have to wake up very early. She closed her eyes and thought about her home. She wondered if she would see her family.

Suddenly she heard a terrible noise from outside. It sounded like a woman laughing and screaming at the same time. It sounded like a crazy person.

Mary whispered, "Stay still. Do not turn on a light. I think it's Rovers."

Jaylin's heart beat faster in her chest. She couldn't catch her breath. She heard people running around in the street outside. A window smashed somewhere. More crazy laughing sounds and a loud crash made Jaylin pull her blankets up a little further.

The Rovers didn't stay around. After a few minutes of yelling and breaking glass they ran past the safe house. One Rover banged on the wall as they passed.

Sierra said, "Let's call the Captain and see if we should stay or leave." She pulled the radio out and called in to the camp.

"I think you will be okay," Captain Ross reassured them. "Rovers don't stay somewhere if they don't think there is anything there for them. Wait for two hours so they are far away and then take off. Drive as fast as you can." Captain Ross didn't sound worried.

Girl Power

5

Two hours later they were speeding away from the safe house. The Rovers were nowhere in sight. They passed a burning building a little way down the road. Jaylin wondered if the Rovers had set it on fire. The sun was starting to come up as they drove into the city. Jaylin thought it was strange to see the city with no lights on and no cars anywhere. Some of the tall buildings she remembered were still there. They all looked like they had been hit with bombs.

Jaylin pulled in front of the other two cars. She drove down the wide main street. There were blown up cars and busses along the sides of the street. The city looked familiar. She knew the streets well. But the streets looked so different without any people on them. The other two cars followed her as she turned off the main street. They made a few more turns and then Jaylin saw a person. She couldn't tell if it was a man or a woman. The person ran across the street and hid in an alley.

Jaylin stopped her car and called to Mary and Sierra on the radio. "Did you guys see that, too?" she asked.

"I did. I think the person is still in that alley. Should we go look?" Sierra asked.

"I will. This is my neighborhood," Jaylin said as she got out of her car. She took her gun with her. She felt scared as she crept towards the alley. She went around the corner, her gun pointed in front of her.

The alley was dark and smelled of things long gone. Before the war, alleys smelled like rotting food. Now they just smelled dark and wet and empty. Deep in the shadows there was a small gasp. Jaylin nearly dropped her gun in fright. "Come out! Come out right now where I can see the sunlight." The person came near and Jaylin saw that she knew her."Mrs. Little?" Jaylin asked. She lowered her gun.

The old lady looked her in the face and smiled. "Oh my God! Jay? Is that really you? I thought you were a soldier! Come here!" The lady stepped towards Jaylin. Jaylin hugged the woman tightly and felt tears come to her eyes. "Jay, is Marcus ok? I think about you kids every day. I always wonder if we did the right thing by sending you to the camp." Mrs. Little looked Jaylin in her eyes. She was excited and nervous to hear the news about her son Marcus.

"Yes, Mrs. Little. Marcus is at the camp with the rest of us. All five of us are there and safe." Jaylin stopped talking and looked at the older woman. She wanted to ask about her parents, but was scared to hear bad news.

"Honey, your Mom is alive. Geraldine and I still live in the church. I can take you to her," Mrs. Little said. Jaylin wanted to ask about her father, but couldn't seem to get out the words.

Jaylin saw Sierra and Mary getting out of their cars. "Mrs. Little, these are my team mates, Sierra and Mary.

We were sent into the city on a mission. Maybe you can help us."

"Please, call me Florence. You are all young women now!" Florence Little shook hands with Sierra and Mary. They locked the cars and walked with her to the church.

6

Florence led the three women around the corner. Jaylin saw her old church halfway down the block. The doors and windows had been covered with wood and metal grates. It looked like a fort. No one could break in. It was a safe place.

They went around to the back of the church and in the back door. Jaylin stopped in the doorway when she saw her mom working in the kitchen in the back of the church.

Geraldine looked up. She stared at her daughter. A look of surprise and relief spread across Geraldine's face. Jaylin hurried towards her mom and the two hugged and sobbed and laughed all at the same time.

Jaylin glanced around the church to see if anyone else was there. "What about Dad?" she asked.

"Honey, I'm so sorry," Geraldine said. "Your dad is gone." Her eyes were filled with tears. "He and Mr. Little went to look for food about a year ago. They never came back. They were killed."

Jaylin looked down at her hands and felt tears in her eyes. She would have to push it out of her mind. She couldn't deal with it now.

"But we are...surviving," Geraldine said. "We learned how to use guns and found a lot of bullets. We stay safe."

They hugged again and then Jaylin introduced everyone. Soon, they all sat down to a meal.

"We have to make do with what we can find," Geraldine said.

"Last spring we made a small garden. That was nice. But someone came and stole all of the food at the end of the summer. Anyway, tell us what happened to you five. We have been so worried!" Florence said.

Jaylin told the two women about what happened since the soldiers took them from the church. The mothers were happy to hear that all five were okay. Mary leaned over and whispered in Jaylin's ear, "We need to find the power cells and get out of here."

"Mom, Florence, we need to find some power cells," Jaylin said. "The Captain thinks they may be in the school."

The two older women looked at each other. "We know where they are," said Florence. "We have them. They're in the basement." Mary, Sierra, and Jaylin looked at each other. How could this trip be so easy? They all ate dinner and felt better with full stomachs. The trip was going well and Jaylin had found her Mom. It was nice to relax in her old church. She felt comfortable.

The three younger women made their beds in the same room on the first floor of the church. It was the old Sunday school room. Jaylin could remember being there for lessons. As she lay and looked out of the window she had a thought. "Guys, can we bring them back to camp?" she asked Mary and Sierra.

The other two sat up and looked at her. "I don't think so," said Mary. "The cars aren't very big, and the camp is already too full."

"I can take my Mom with me. Florence can go with one of you. The power cells can go with the other," Jaylin said. "I can't just leave them here." She thought about her Mom in the empty church and her Dad who was killed.

"We can't take them," said Mary firmly.

Jaylin was starting to feel angry. "If we can't bring them with us, I'll have to stay here," she said.

Mary and Sierra looked at each other. "I'm sorry you feel that way," Sierra said.

7

The next morning Jaylin woke up to the smell of waffles. She ran into the kitchen and saw her Mom laughing with Mary and Sierra. "Why did you let me sleep so late?" Jaylin asked. The sun was fully up. She had not slept so late in years.

"You needed to sleep," said her mom. "These girls are telling me all about your camp. It sounds nice. But I think your job is too dangerous."

Jaylin smiled. "Then I guess I will have to stay here and help you and Florence. Where is she?"

"She's getting eggs. We have a chicken coop not too far away," said her mom.

Just then Florence came in the door. "I found 11 eggs! It almost feels like they knew we had company!" She was happy and smiling as she put the eggs on the counter.

"Jaylin, I have news for you," said Mary. "Sierra and I talked about it this morning. We want to try to bring your Mom and Florence back to camp. We will come up with a way to talk to Captain Ross about it."

All five women felt happy as they ate a very good breakfast of waffles and eggs. They spent the day packing the power cells in the car and looking for anything they could take back. Mary's car was full of cargo. The power cells were put into the special rack that went on top of Mary's car. Florence would go in Sierra's car, and Geraldine would travel with her daughter.

They had an early dinner and went to bed. They were going to go before dawn and try to get to camp in one day. With all of the cargo and extra weight they would have to drive slowly. As they got into the cars the next morning, Jaylin looked around her. This might be the last time she ever saw her neighborhood.

Then she realized that she was happy to go back to camp. Camp was home now. She wanted to get back quickly. She missed her twin brother.

The three cars were out of the city by the time the sun came up. They turned their radios on and talked back and forth as they drove. It felt so safe to be talking and laughing. Almost like old times. Florence and Geraldine told stories about Marcus, Jaylin, and Jonah. Mary and Sierra laughed at the silly things they had done.

All of the sudden there was a loud noise. Smoke and dust filled the air. Jaylin could not see. She sped up to get out of the dust cloud. She slammed on her brakes and jumped out of her car with her gun in front of her.

Sierra's car stopped next to her. Sierra jumped out and pointed her gun into the dust cloud. They could not see Mary's car.

"Mary!" screamed Sierra. "Mary! Where are you?"

Jaylin turned back to her car and grabbed her First Aid pack. She had a flashlight in there and she turned it on. The light shone into the dust and smoke but still she could not see anything. She walked straight back to where she thought Mary was. Mary's car was upside down. The cargo was scattered all over the road. Mary was stuck in the car. Her seatbelt kept her in the seat.

Jaylin could see a gash on Mary's head. Blood was all over the inside of the glass. Jaylin called for Sierra. They carefully opened the door. Mary groaned. Her eyes opened for a second and then closed. Jaylin held Mary while Sierra undid the seatbelt. They carried Mary back to the cars and laid her down. She had cuts all over her face and arms. She did not open her eyes.

"Use the radio to call camp," said Geraldine.

"The radio was in her car. I doubt it works anymore," Sierra said as she looked down at her sister.

Jaylin thought Sierra looked like a statue. She was still and pale. Her voice was flat and she had no emotion.

"What happened?" asked Geraldine.

"It was a bomb left from the war. Mary must have driven over it," Sierra said. She was standing still looking down at her sister.

"Mom is right though. We need to call camp. What can we do?" Jaylin asked.

"We can't get all five of us into two cars," Sierra said.

"Yes we can. We can leave all of the stuff," Florence said.

Sierra and Jaylin looked at each other. Captain

Ross would be very angry with them if they did not bring the power cells. Had those even survived the crash? The smoke from the explosion was clearing up. They could see the junk left from the car. Pieces of cargo were scattered everywhere.

Florence went into the smoke and dust. "Look over here!" she called out. "I found the power cells!"

Jaylin ran over to Florence. The case that held the power cells was not broken. She opened the case and saw the power cells tucked inside safely. She locked the case. She asked Florence, "Can you squeeze into the car with Mom?"

"Absolutely. Yes. How long is the drive?" asked Florence.

"We have a few more hours. These cars can't go fast even when they are empty," Jaylin said.

Florence and Geraldine pulled all of their clothes and bags out of the back of the two cars. The four of them used clothes and blankets to make a bed for Mary. They carefully lifted her into the back of Sierra's car. They used more blankets to keep her from sliding around. They attached the power cells to the top of Sierra's car.

The two women could barely fit behind Jaylin in the cargo space. As soon as everyone was inside the cars, Sierra and Jaylin drove off as fast as they could. They could not talk to each other because the radio was broken. They drove next to each other the whole way.

The sun was setting when they finally saw the wire fence and the warehouse that hid the door to their camp.

8

Suddenly, Jaylin saw movement from her right side. A small group of people came quickly towards them. One of them ran ahead of the rest. He was running next to Jaylin's car. He had empty, black eyes. He looked right at Jaylin through the window and growled. His hair was long and knotted. He was missing teeth and a part of his nose. A long red scar covered his arm.

"Rovers!" Jaylin screamed. She drove as fast as she could towards the gate. They could see the doors of the warehouse opening. Inside of the warehouse were soldiers. The soldiers ran out to the sides of the doors and started shooting at the Rovers. Jaylin and Sierra sped into the warehouse. They heard shots and screams from behind them. The doors slammed shut as they stopped their cars. "

Mary's been hurt!" Sierra shouted as she climbed out of her car. Soldiers came running towards her. Jaylin and the two mothers climbed out of her car.

Captain Ross ran to Jaylin. "What happened?" he demanded. Jaylin told him about the explosion. She showed him the power cells. "But who are these women?" asked Captain Ross.

"We should go to your office," said Jaylin.

They watched as the nurses came and took Mary away. Sierra walked behind them. She did not look at Jaylin as she passed. Jaylin saw that she was still very pale. They followed Captain Ross down to his office. He closed the door behind them and sat at his desk.

He looked at Jaylin and put his hands on the desk in front of him. "You came back with a badly injured teammate and two civilians," he said quietly.

Scared to make Captain Ross angry, Jaylin explained the whole trip. The Captain listened quietly and asked her questions. "So you want to let these two women stay?" he asked her when she was done.

"Yes sir. They will not survive alone much longer outside. The Rovers are braver now. You saw the attack that just happened. It could happen again." Jaylin was surprised by how calm she was. She thought she should be nervous asking the Captain to let her Mom stay. But it was the right thing to do. She felt brave.

"I have to discuss it with the Commander," said Captain Ross. "While you are waiting to hear from me, they can stay with you."

Girl Power

9

Jaylin took her Mom and Florence down to the cafe. It was empty. A few plates had been left out for late snacks. They took some and sat down. "Wait here for a minute. I'll be right back," Jaylin said. She ran down the hall to her room. Jonah was sitting on his bed. "Come with me. Right now!" Jaylin said. She ran out of the room and pounded on Marcus' door. Leila and Mike were with him. "Hurry! Come with me!" she called to them. All five of them went back to the cafe.

Marcus stopped in the middle of the room when he saw his mom. "Mom!" he yelled and ran towards her.

The seven people stayed up all night talking. The younger people asked about everyone they knew. Leila and Mike found out that their family had all escaped to a farm in the north. Only Mr. Little, Florence, and Jaylin's parents had stayed at the church. "We stayed because we thought you might come back. You know where your home is," said Geraldine.

Jaylin reached across the table to her Mom and held her hand. It felt so nice to hear her voice.

"Home is where the heart is, Mom. I'm just glad that you're here," Jonah said as he hugged his mom.

10

It took two days for Captain Ross to finally talk to Jonah, Jaylin, and Marcus. "The Commander and I want to know what skills these women have. How can they help the camp?" Captain Ross asked.

"My Mom is an excellent cook, sir," said Jonah. "Florence knows how to take care of animals."

"I think they will make people feel hopeful," said Jaylin. "It's been a long time since we talked to other people."

Captain Ross looked at the three of them. He gave them a small smile. "We are going to let them stay. They will have to work with everyone else. We are very happy that Jaylin brought back the power cells. Thank you," the Captain said. Then he left the room.

The three of them looked at each other. They all had huge smiles on their faces. "Woo-hoo!" shouted Marcus. "Let's go tell them!" He took off down the hallway. Jaylin and Jonah walked behind him. Jaylin felt very proud. Since she had brought the power cells back, she was getting a reward. Because of her success, her mom would be able to stay.

"I'm proud of you, little sis," said Jonah.

"What do you mean by little? We were born at the same time!" Jaylin said.

"I figure since I'm a few minutes older. I am more mature than you," Jonah said with a smile.

Jaylin punched him in his arm. "Well, I know who can tell us which one is right!" Jaylin said. She took off running behind Marcus.

11

Jaylin went to see Mary in the hospital the next day. Mary had finally woken up from two days in a coma. The doctor said that she would get better. Right now, she needed to stay still.

"Hey Jaylin," Mary said. "How are you? How is your Mom?"

"I'm okay. My Mom is going to stay. So is Florence. How are you?" Jaylin asked.

"They were able to set the bones. In a month I should be okay again. You guys got me here in time." Mary looked very pale and weak in her bed. "Where's Sierra?" she asked.

"She hasn't been here yet?" Jaylin asked.

"No. I haven't seen her since I woke up," said Mary.

"I'll check on her when I leave," said Jaylin. How come Sierra hadn't visited her sister yet?

Jaylin and Mary talked about the explosion and the trip. Jaylin told Mary about the Rovers that tried to attack them in front of the camp. She described how the Rover had looked at her. "I can't stop thinking about his eyes. It was like he wasn't a human," said Jaylin.

"I overheard some people talking last night. They said that a group of Rovers has been outside of the camp waiting for the door to open all week. Most of them were shot when we drove in. Jaylin, I'm scared." Mary looked at Jaylin with big eyes.

"Me too. If they get in, we will have to fight them," Jaylin said.

Mary was tired. Jaylin left to look for Sierra. She knocked on the door of Sierra's room. No answer. She tried the doorknob. The door was unlocked. Jaylin felt strange going into another person's room. But she was worried. She leaned her head in. There was a terrible smell. It was like someone had not taken a bath in days.

"Sierra?" Jaylin asked the dark room. Jaylin turned on the switch. Light filled the small space. Sierra was sitting on the floor. She stared at Jaylin. She looked like she needed a shower. Jaylin met Sierra's eyes. They were blank and empty. Jaylin had seen eyes like that before. The Rover had looked at her with a similar set.

"What do you want?" asked Sierra in the same flat voice she had spoken in when Mary's car blew up. "Why are you here?"

"I wanted to see if you were okay. Mary's awake. She's asking for you," Jaylin said.

"Get out," said Sierra. She grabbed Jaylin's arm and pushed her out of the room. Sierra began screaming and laughing at Jaylin. She didn't sound human.

Jonah ran down the hall towards them. He must have heard the noise. Sierra just kept screaming and laughing. "What's happened to her?" Jonah asked.

Jaylin didn't want to say what she was thinking, that she looked just like the crazy Rovers. "I'm not sure," Jaylin whispered. Jonah and Jaylin agreed to take Sierra to the hospital. They left Sierra with the doctors. "I think it will be a long time until Sierra is normal," said Jaylin. She was scared about what might happen in the future.

"Come on, Sis. Let's go get Mom. You can't help Sierra now." Jonah put an arm around her shoulders. They walked to the door. Jaylin thought Jonah was right. This was not a thing she could fix. But she would do anything to keep camp safe. This was her home. This was where her family was.

About The Author

Kitty Heite is a trained Special Education instructor and foster parent of teens in Philadelphia. Both of these experiences have informed her understanding of the needs of older youth and young adults struggling to engage with reading. She dedicates this story to Gloria.

Girl Power

About The Publisher

Story Shares is a nonprofit focused on supporting the millions of teens and adults who struggle with reading by creating a new shelf in the library specifically for them. The ever-growing collection features content that is compelling and culturally relevant for teens and adults, yet still readable at a range of lower reading levels.

Story Shares generates content by engaging deeply with writers, bringing together a community to create this new kind of book. With more intriguing and approachable stories to choose from, the teens and adults who have fallen behind are improving their skills and beginning to discover the joy of reading. For more information, visit storyshares.org.

Easy to Read. Hard to Put Down.